ON THE CASE!

FBI AGENTS

Madison Capitano

I0892773

Rourke Educational Media
A Division of Carson Dellosa Education

ROURKE'S
SCHOOL to HOME
CONNECTIONS

BEFORE AND DURING READING ACTIVITIES

Before Reading: *Building Background Knowledge and Vocabulary*

Building background knowledge can help children process new information and build upon what they already know. Before reading a book, it is important to tap into what children already know about the topic. This will help them develop their vocabulary and increase their reading comprehension.

Questions and Activities to Build Background Knowledge:

1. Look at the front cover of the book and read the title. What do you think this book will be about?
2. What do you already know about this topic?
3. Take a book walk and skim the pages. Look at the table of contents, photographs, captions, and bold words. Did these text features give you any information or predictions about what you will read in this book?

Vocabulary: *Vocabulary Is Key to Reading Comprehension*

Use the following directions to prompt a conversation about each word.

- Read the vocabulary words.
- What comes to mind when you see each word?
- What do you think each word means?

Vocabulary Words:

- *cold cases*
- *informants*
- *notoriously*
- *polygraph*
- *profiling*
- *psychology*

During Reading: *Reading for Meaning and Understanding*

To achieve deep comprehension of a book, children are encouraged to use close reading strategies. During reading, it is important to have children stop and make connections. These connections result in deeper analysis and understanding of a book.

Close Reading a Text

During reading, have children stop and talk about the following:

- Any confusing parts
- Any unknown words
- Text to text, text to self, text to world connections
- The main idea in each chapter or heading

Encourage children to use context clues to determine the meaning of any unknown words. These strategies will help children learn to analyze the text more thoroughly as they read.

When you are finished reading this book, turn to the next-to-last page for **After Reading Questions** and an **Activity**.

CENE DO NOT CROSS • CRIME SCENE DO NOT CROSS • CRIME SCENE DO NOT CROSS • CRIM

TABLE OF CONTENTS

ON THE CASE

Agents for the Federal Bureau of Investigation (FBI) make sure that people follow the law. They solve crimes and arrest criminals. They are like police officers for the federal government!

CAUTION DO NOT ENTER CAUTION

FBI agents must pass a **polygraph** test before they are hired. Agents keep people safe. They can't hide anything that could stop them from doing their jobs!

THE TRUTH TEST

Polygraph machines are also called lie detectors. They are useful, but not accepted as evidence in court. Some people can trick the machine into thinking they are telling the truth.

» **polygraph** (PAH-lee-graf): a machine that detects physical evidence that someone is telling a lie, such as a change in heart rate

A THIEF IN THE NIGHT

One morning, an art museum director finds that four famous paintings are missing. It's a terrible loss! Don't worry, an FBI agent is on the case.

The Art Crime Team sometimes meets with experts for more training.

In 2004, the FBI created an Art Crime Team for cases just like this one. Stolen art is **notoriously** hard to track down, but this team is dedicated.

They've recovered more than 15,000 items!

» **notoriously** (noh-TOR-ee-uhs-lee): widely known for being bad or difficult

The Art Crime Team studies art history. They study how people sell art so they can find stolen works when they show up for sale. In this case, the Art Crime Team set a trap. The thief was quickly caught, and the paintings were returned to the museum.

STILL AT LARGE

Thirteen paintings were stolen from the Isabella Stewart Gardner Museum in Boston, Massachusetts, in 1990. No one has been caught and none of the paintings have been found. The museum is offering a ten-million-dollar reward for information leading to the recovery of all the paintings in good condition.

The empty frames of the stolen paintings are still hanging in the Isabella Stewart Gardner Museum.

KILLER ON THE LOOSE

A dangerous criminal has killed several people in the past few weeks. They may have killed before. They need to be caught as quickly as possible. An FBI agent is on the case!

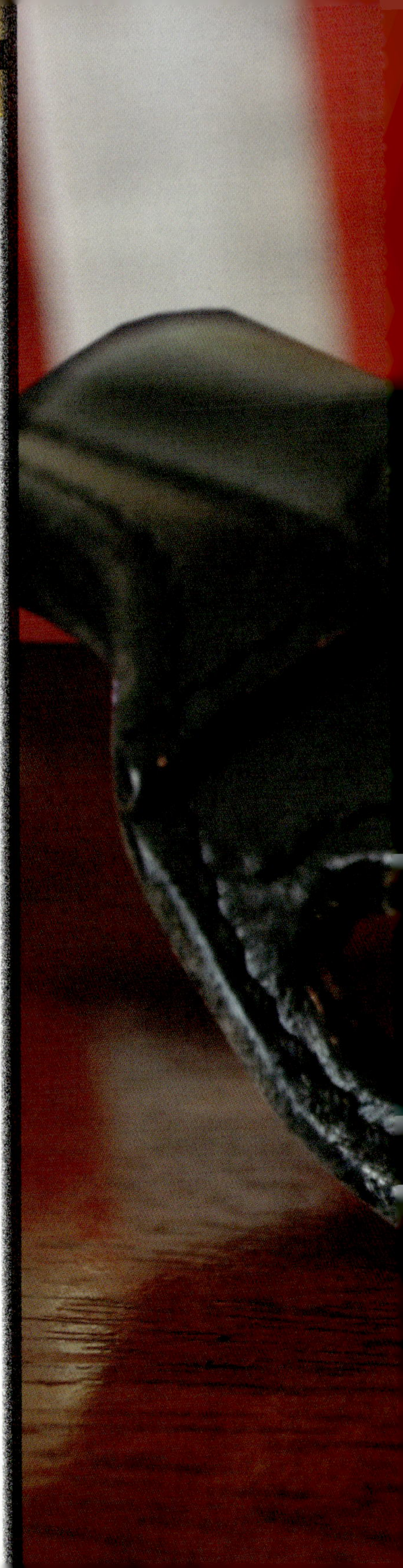

FEDERAL
BUREAU OF
INVESTIGATION
U S
DEPARTMENT OF
JUSTICE

Some FBI agents work just like detectives. They find evidence, investigate crimes, and put criminals in jail. The Behavioral Analysis Unit (BAU) works this way. These agents use criminal **profiling** to help solve cases.

STAR STUDDED

The BAU stars in the television show *Criminal Minds*. Not everything on the show is fake! Some episodes are based on real FBI cases.

» **profiling** (PROH-fye-ling): using reasoning and information about traits and tendencies to figure out what an unknown person might be like

Teams in the BAU use case histories, scientific evidence, and **psychology** to try to understand the behavior of criminals. They do this to predict what criminals might do next, and to solve crimes that have already been committed.

» **psychology** (sye-KAH-luh-jee): the study of the human mind, human emotions, and human behavior

In this case, the BAU team used computers to analyze many case studies. They found some connections to **cold cases**. They used new technology and old evidence to link the cases and find the identity of the killer.

» **cold cases** (kohld KASE-ez): unsolved criminal cases that have stopped being actively investigated because of a lack of evidence

ORGANIZED CRIME CATCHERS

When an important businessperson goes missing, police think it might be the work of organized criminals. Organized crime—also known as "the mob" or "the mafia"—is a system of people who work together to break the law. Don't fear, FBI agents are on the case!

FBI agents may spend many hours secretly watching crime organizations to gather evidence.

FBI agents are responsible for bringing organized criminals to justice. They use many tools such as **informants**, electronic spying, and undercover operations. FBI agents can get a lot of very important information by pretending to be on the wrong side of the law.

» **informants** (in-FORM-uhnts): people who give information about illegal activities to the authorities

Organized crime sources helped FBI agents figure out that the businessperson disappeared for a completely different reason. The person had stolen money from their company and was trying to get away while the FBI looked the other way. Not a chance!

TAKE A BOW

Joseph Pistone was a great undercover FBI agent. The mafia even offered a reward for his death. They never found him, though. Joseph Pistone helped convict more than 100 organized criminals.

Joseph Pistone used a fake name when he was undercover. He went by Donnie Brasco.

FBI agents are on duty all over the United States to handle many different kinds of crimes. They train, study, and work hard to keep ahead of criminals and put them behind bars. FBI agents are on the case!

MEMORY GAME

Look at the pictures. What do you remember reading on the pages where each image appeared?

INDEX

AFTER READING QUESTIONS

1. What are two jobs an FBI agent can have?
2. What is the name of the FBI team that finds stolen art?
3. How many paintings are missing from the Isabella Stewart Gardner Museum?
4. What kind of test do agents have to take to be hired?
5. If you were an FBI agent, what kind of job would you want?

ACTIVITY

It's time to create a new identity! You're an FBI agent going undercover to spy on suspected criminals. You need a new name, a new history, and new identification. To get ready for your mission, create an ID card and documents that explain who you are.

ABOUT THE AUTHOR

Madison Capitano is a writer in Columbus, Ohio, who loves to watch mystery shows! She thinks the FBI is pretty cool and loves to read about the amazing things they've done. Madison used to read books to her little brother and sister all the time. Now she loves to write books for other kids to enjoy.

© 2021 Rourke Educational Media

All rights reserved. No part of this book may be reproduced or utilized in any form or by any means, electronic or mechanical including photocopying, recording, or by any information storage and retrieval system without permission in writing from the publisher.

www.rourkeeducationalmedia.com

PHOTO CREDITS: page 1: ©AndreyPopov / iStock; page 5: ©Federal Bureau of Investigation / FBI.gov; page 6: ©standret / iStock; page 9: ©Alexander Sviridov / iStock; page 10: ©Federal Bureau of Investigation / FBI.gov; page 13: ©Federal Bureau of Investigation / Wikimedia; page 15: ©Everett Collection / Newscom; page 16: ©Federal Bureau of Investigation / FBI.gov; page 19: ©JohnnyGreig / iStock; page 20: ©avid_creative / iStock; page 23: ©Lorado / iStock; page 24: ©innovatedcaptures / iStock; page 27: ©Federal Bureau of Investigation / FBI.gov; page 28: ©Nes / iStock; caution tape: ©tcenitelkrasoti / Pixabay; magnifying glass: ©Pixaline / Pixabay

Edited by: Kim Thompson
Cover design by: Kathy Walsh
Interior design by: Sara Radka

Library of Congress PCN Data

FBI Agents / Madison Capitano
(On the Case!)
ISBN 978-1-73163-819-9 (hard cover)
ISBN 978-1-73163-896-0 (soft cover)
ISBN 978-1-73163-973-8 (e-Book)
ISBN 978-1-73164-050-5 (e-Pub)
Library of Congress Control Number: 2020930243

Rourke Educational Media
Printed in the United States of America
01-1942011937